The
Night Before
Christmas

By R. Schuyler Hooke
Illustrated by Richard Courtney

A GOLDEN BOOK • NEW YORK

CREATED BY BRITT ALLCROFT
Thomas the Tank Engine & Friends™

Based on The Railway Series by The Reverend W Awdry.
© 2013 Gullane (Thomas) LLC.
Thomas the Tank Engine & Friends and Thomas & Friends are trademarks of Gullane (Thomas) Limited.
HIT and the HIT Entertainment logo are trademarks of HIT Entertainment Limited.
All rights reserved. Published in the United States by Golden Books, an imprint of Random House Children's Books,
a division of Penguin Random House LLC, 1745 Broadway, New York, NY 10019, and in Canada by Random House
of Canada, a division of Penguin Random House Ltd., Toronto. Golden Books, A Golden Book, A Little Golden Book,
the G colophon, and the distinctive spine design are registered
trademarks of Penguin Random House LLC.
randomhousekids.com
www.thomasandfriends.com
ISBN 978-0-449-81663-9 (trade) — ISBN 978-0-449-81664-6 (ebook)
Printed in the United States of America
16 15 14 13 12 11 10 9 8
Random House Children's Books supports the First Amendment and celebrates the right to read.

'Twas the night before Christmas, and all through the Yard
The engines were restless, and sleeping was hard.

Their stockings—still empty, from the
glimpses they stole—
Would soon, they all hoped, be brimming
with coal.

Percy was dreaming (his smile, it was bright)
Of a shiny new headlamp to guide him at night.

Even Sir Topham had stayed in the Shed
With thoughts of Christmas awhirl in
his head.

Then, out in the Yard, there arose such
a clatter!
Soon all were awake to see what was
the matter.

Out rolled the engines on the rails in the floor
As Sir Topham himself threw open the door.

The moon shining bright on the new-fallen snow
Made night seem like day to the engines below.

And what to nine pairs of eyes should appear,
But a miniature sleigh and eight tiny reindeer.

And the little old driver—who was surely
St. Nick—
    He didn't look well. In fact, he looked sick.

His reindeer were gliding but seemed
to be slow,
    And the driver mumbled the names
that we know:

"Now, Dasher! Now, Dancer! Now, Prancer and Vixen . . .

This old elf has the flu. . . . Oh, my! I need fixin'!

To the top of the shed! To the top of the wall!

We've got to land quickly. Oh, darn! Dash it all!"

So down to the Yard the eight of them
dropped,
    And the sleigh and the driver and reindeer
all stopped.

St. Nick's cheeks were red, but something
seemed funny. . . .
His eyes didn't sparkle; his nose, it
was runny.

"Sir Topham," he said, a sad look on his face,
"I cannot go on. You must take my place."

Sir Hatt shook his head. "I can't, for I fear
While I know about trains, I know nothing
of deer."

"Trains are perfect," said Nick. "I'm sure they'll do fine.
Bust your buffers, my friends, and get in a line."

And faster than diesels the engines they came.

Santa whistled a new list, and called each by name:

"Now, Thomas! Now, Percy! Now, Gordon—James, too!

Edward and Henry! Bill! Ben! I need you!

"These toys must be taken to each girl and boy.
I know you can do it. Deliver great joy!"

Nick turned to Sir Topham and said, "One thing more.
Your dress coat won't do—it's really a bore."
He pulled out a red one, and to no one's surprise,
That coat, it turned out to be just the right size.

And now you would bet that St. Nick had
a twin,
Except for the beard on one rounded chin.
And while Nick wore a cap trimmed with fur
on his head,
Sir Topham Hatt's top hat had holly instead.

But night was still passing as children all
slept,
So, giving a nod, up Sir Topham Hatt leapt.
As the engines gained speed, seeming almost
to fly,
From his seat in the sleigh, Sir Hatt gave a
loud cry:

"My friends, we are needed. I'm feeling quite fine.
We'll be Really Useful, and—yes—
Right on Time!"

So all across Sodor they raced on their way,
    Eight steaming engines pulling one gift-filled
sleigh.
    And we heard on the wind as they puffed out
of sight,
    "Merry Christmas to all, and to all
a good night!"